# The Little Helmet

# by Nicholas Pavitt

Copyright © 2015 Nicholas Pavitt

Cover design, text and illustrations by Nicholas Pavitt.

All rights reserved.

ISBN-10: 1506193293
ISBN-13: 978-1506193298

Across Hatland television pictures were suddenly interrupted by the picture of a news reporter saying, "This is a newsflash! We bring reports that a terrifying dragon has been seen flying over Hatland."

At that moment the dragon dived out of the sky towards where the reporter was standing, breathing fire as it went. The dragon missed the terrified reporter and rose high into the sky.

" That was close, " gulped the reporter. "Well there you are, as I speak, Hatland is being attacked by a dragon. Hatland's fire brigade say they can do little to stop the creature. So, is there anyone who can save Hatland? Wooah, here it comes again!"

The terrified newsreporter ran for cover, along with the camera crew as the newsflash ended.

Amongst the flags and shields in Hatland's castle, the King and Queen walked up and down, trying to think of a way to save their beloved Hatland.

"I know, dearest Queen," said the King, clicking his fingers as he spoke, "Hatricks the magician could stop that dragon with his magic."

So, Hatricks was called to see the King and Queen. In he came carrying his wand and a crystal ball, doing his best not to trip over his long beard as he walked.

"Hatricks," the King asked, " could you use your magic to stop the dragon?"

Hatricks looked into his crystal ball, where a dragon breathing smoke and fire could be seen. Shaking his head Hatricks replied, "Um, I could not get close enough. Long distance magic is not safe, I'm sorry."

Now all three began to walk up and down, trying to think of a way to stop the dragon.

"Dearest King, I know!" shouted the Queen, "We could call the knights on a quest to stop this dragon, just like in the days of old."

Both the King and Hatricks thought that this was a good idea.

And so, the knights of Hatland were called to the castle, each with their brightly coloured shields.

With the great and the good of Hatland before them the King and Queen told the knights of the quest to capture the dragon.

"Which of our brave knights shall save Hatland?" asked the King.

The knights looked at one another and remembering the television pictures of the dragon, remained quiet.

"No takers!" said the Queen turning to the King, "Well then, all Hatland is doomed."

Just as the King and Queen began to give up hope of saving Hatland, a fuss could be heard at the back of the throne room.

There stood two guards holding a tiny battered helmet, carrying a battered sword and shield. With everyone looking at them the guards tried to explain, "This little one saw the television pictures of the dragon and came to help. We were just trying to remove the little whipper-snapper, your Highnesses."

"Well as no other knight wants to stop the dragon, we may need your help," said the Queen and with this the guards quickly let go of the little helmet.

"Your Highnesses, I will brave every danger to become the best knight in all Hatland. I shall catch this dragon!" chirped the little helmet cheerfully.

"My you are brave," the Queen replied approvingly.

"Well, before you set off," said the King, "our stables will give you one of our finest horses, and Hatricks will give you something to help your quest."

As the King said this everyone turned to watch Hatricks whisper some magic words and begin to wave his magic wand.

Everyone watching wondered what the magician would magic up.

They thought he might magic up something like a magic sword, a lucky charm, a magic potion or a fireproof shield.

There was a flash of magic, and what appeared before the crowd...

a magic flask and magic sandwiches!

"At least you will not get hungry," explained Hatricks.

The little helmet rode across the countryside, with the magic flask and sandwiches.

How long the quest would last the little helmet was not sure, but he knew he would succeed.

Through village after village he travelled, hearing tales of the dragon from Hatpeople who had had narrow escapes.

Then, late in the afternoon, a group of Hatpeople ran up to him, telling him not to go any further for the dragon was in their village.

At this even the little helmet's horse began to worry.

"This is my quest my friends, you have nothing to fear for soon your village and all Hatland shall be safe," said the brave little helmet as he rode into the village.

The little helmet found the dragon sitting all alone by the village well.

As he got off his horse and walked up to the dragon, he saw that the dragon was crying, great big dragon's tears.

As the little helmet got nearer to the dragon, he held his shield above his head to stop himself from getting wet.

"What's up?" asked the little helmet.

The sad dragon sniffed, and looking down replied, " It's not fair, everyone's run away. All I wanted was some friends to play with, and they have all run off."

"I'm not surprised, everyone is afraid of your fire."

"Oh, I'm sorry about that, it's all I'm good at is fire. But you're not frightened of me, are you?"

"Who me? No. I'm not frightened of anything, especially dragons who just want to be friends. I tell you what, I'm hungry, and I bet you could do with something to eat."

"Oh, yes please!" answered a delighted dragon.

The little helmet shared the sandwiches between the two of them. They were the dragon's favourite magic sandwiches. As they tucked in the little helmet asked, " What do you say, friends?"

"Me friends with you?" replied the happy dragon.

"Well, me and the rest of Hatland. You could live at the castle, take part in royal parades, and help with the odd barbecue even. You would be a star, and you would have no end of friends, we would all get along fine."

"Oh that's fantastic, how soon can we go?" the dragon asked as it gulped down the last of the sandwiches.

As the little helmet and the dragon made their way back, everybody at the castle was wondering what had happened to the little helmet. Hatricks looked into his crystal ball, but all he could see were clouds of smoke.

"We are doomed," said the King as he began to walk up and down once more.

"Now, now," said the Queen, "Don't think like that my dearest King. Our brave little helmet will save Hatland, and become our greatest knight. Hey, we don't even know his name, and all the other knights are called Sir something or other. So what shall we call this one when he returns ?"

Suddenly shouts of "Surprise! Surprise!" could be heard from the back of the room.

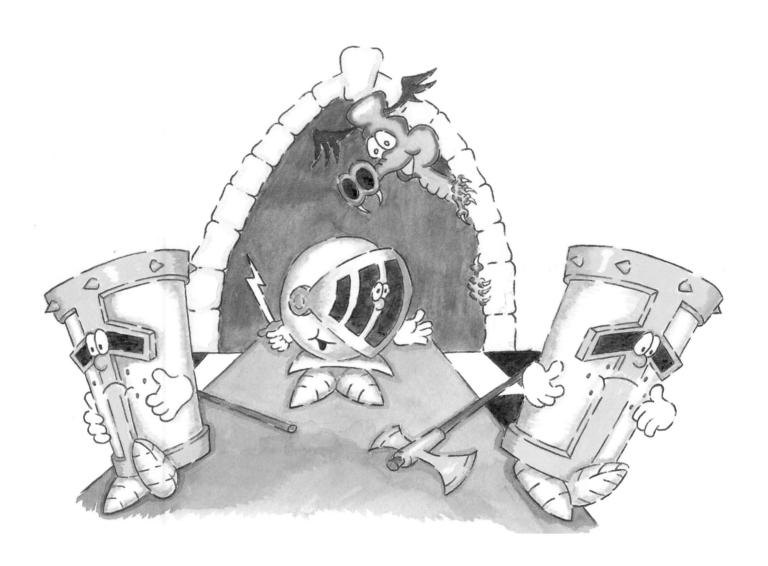

"Sir Prize, that's a good name," said the Queen as the triumphant little helmet and the dragon burst into the room.

On seeing the dragon inside the castle the two terrified guards were the first to run and hide.

It was some time before everyone believed that the dragon just wanted to be friends. When the King and Queen came out from behind their thrones they knighted the little helmet straight away.

And as they finished saying, "Arise Sir Prize", Hatricks tried a touch of magic. With one wave of his magic wand the throne room was filled with a flash of golden light.

When the light had gone, where once had stood the battered little helmet, now stood a wonderous golden helmet. The little helmet was now known as Sir Prize the bravest knight in all Hatland, friend to all, especially dragons!

12849180R00016

Printed in Great Britain
by Amazon.co.uk, Ltd.,
Marston Gate.